Have an Abominably Good Day

Eric T. Krackow

4880 Lower Valley Road · Atglen, Pennsylvania 19310

Schiffer Books are available at special discounts for bulk purchases for sales promotions or premiums. Special editions, including personalized covers, corporate imprints, and excerpts can be created in large quantities for special needs. For more information contact the publisher:

Published by Schiffer Publishing Ltd.
4880 Lower Valley Road
Atglen, PA 19310
Phone: (610) 593-1777; Fax: (610) 593-2002
E-mail: Info@schifferbooks.com

For the largest selection of fine reference books on this and related subjects, please visit our web site at **www.schifferbooks.com**
We are always looking for people to write books on new and related subjects. If you have an idea for a book please contact us at the above address.

This book may be purchased from the publisher.
Include $5.00 for shipping.
Please try your bookstore first.
You may write for a free catalog.

In Europe, Schiffer books are distributed by
Bushwood Books
6 Marksbury Ave.
Kew Gardens
Surrey TW9 4JF England
Phone: 44 (0) 20 8392 8585; Fax: 44 (0) 20 8392 9876
E-mail: info@bushwoodbooks.co.uk
Website: www.bushwoodbooks.co.uk

Sometimes the most important gifts are the ones from the heart.

Dedicated to my wife, Heather.

At the end of a wintry day, not so very long ago, a large, white creature named Abe sat all alone on the top of a steep hill. Below him he could see a snow-covered forest and the animals that lived in it.

His long, furry legs dangled over the edge of the hill as he watched the flurry of activity on the forest floor. It was Christmas Eve and all of his forest friends were busy decorating the trees with shiny ornaments, candy-canes, garland, and other holiday things. They all looked so happy.

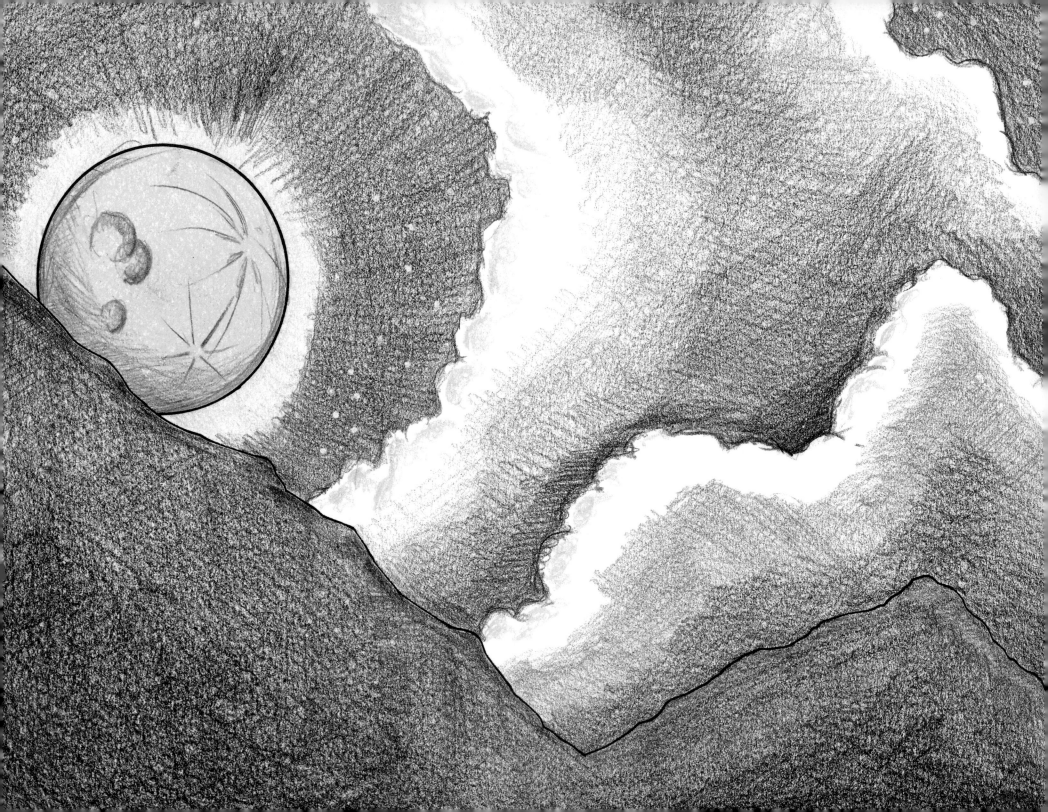

You would think that this would be a happy time for Abe, too, but it was not. One look at Abe's big blue eyes told you that he was very sad. You see, Abe had a problem. Every Christmas Eve, this large Abominable Snowman would accidentally do something to mess things up.

Once, when he wasn't watching where he was going, he stepped on all the Christmas presents stacked underneath the tree.

Another time, he got tied up in the Christmas lights and broke most of the bulbs while trying to get them untangled. And then, just last year, he broke the Christmas tree in half when he tried to put the star on the top! He felt awful.

"This year will be different," he thought. "This year I won't ruin Christmas for everyone." So Abe stood up from his hillside perch and started out on a long walk into the forest...alone.

At the same time, in a small town at the other end of the forest, the children were playing in the snow. They were having great fun. Jill and Timmy were building a snowman, while Billy and his sister, Hannah, were having a friendly snowball fight.

The children always enjoyed playing together, especially in the snow, and they were having a wonderful time. That is, until Billy went too far.

Hannah and Billy had been playing for a long time and Hannah wanted to go home so their mom could make them hot cocoa. But Billy wasn't ready to stop. "C'mon, Hannah!" he yelled. "Try hitting me with your best shot!"

"That's okay, Billy," Hannah answered. "I'm starting to get really cold and I'm ready to go home ."

"We're getting tired, too," Jill agreed. "Timmy and I are going inside."

"But I want to play," Billy shouted. "It's still early and I'm having fun!" Billy was growing angry. He did not want to go home yet and didn't want his friends to go home either.

Sometimes, when Billy was upset, he would do things that he knew he shouldn't. As Hannah turned to go home, Billy scooped up a big clump of snow, made it into a large snowball, and threw it at her as hard as he could. The snowball hit Hannah in the back of the head and hurt so much that she started to cry.

Hannah didn't say anything. She just cried softly and walked into the woods. The snowball had hurt her feelings more than her head, and she wanted to be alone. Billy stood and watched his sister disappear into the trees. As he thought about how he had treated her, the smile slowly vanished from his face.

In the forest, Hannah walked for a very long time. She was upset by what her brother had done. "How could he be so mean?" she thought.

Pieces of the snowball were still in her scarf. They were cold and wet on her neck, so she took off the scarf and shook them out.

She was wrapping it back around her neck when, all of a sudden, she slipped on some ice and fell to the ground. She tried to get up, but the snow under her feet began to crumble and give way. Before she knew it, she was sliding down a huge and very steep hill!

Trees and rocks went whizzing past her as she swooshed down the snowy slope. After what seemed like a very long time, she finally came to a stop when she hit something. It didn't hurt. Whatever it was, it was soft...and big.

Hannah slowly stood up and looked up at the thing in front of her. Oddly enough, the thing was looking back at her!

She couldn't believe her eyes. It was a huge creature, at least ten feet tall. It was all covered in white fur and had two big blue eyes. All Hannah could do was sit there and stare... and Abe just stood and stared back at her.

They had studied each other for quite a little while, when Abe slowly moved toward Hannah and knelt down. Frightened, Hannah curled up into a ball and covered her eyes. She was sure he wanted to hurt her!

But nothing happened. After a few seconds she dared to open her eyes and saw that her scarf was in his hand. It had come off when she fell and he just wanted to give it back to her.

Hannah felt badly for
thinking the worst of him
and gently took the scarf
out of his large hand.

"My name is Hannah," she said, though she was still a little bit afraid. "What's your name?"

The creature smiled and bent down to shake hands with his new friend. "A-Abe," he answered in a deep, monstrous voice.

All at once Hannah knew she was safe with Abe. "Can you help me?" she asked. "My brother and I got into an argument earlier and I went for a walk in the forest to calm down. But then I fell down the hill and now I'm lost. Can you show me how to get back to the town? My mom's at home making hot cocoa." Just then a little tear formed in the corner of her eye.

Abe wiped her tear away with his large finger and nodded at her. He knew that, if he were lost, he would want someone to help him find his way home. Abe pointed to his shoulders and motioned for Hannah to climb aboard.

Abe held her legs while Hannah held his neck. Abe then stood up as high as he could. Hannah had never been up so high. Sitting on his shoulders, she could see more of the forest than she had ever seen before. But she didn't see what was most important to her. "I can't see my house, Abe," she said. "Is there some place higher than here?"

A big smile formed on
Abe's furry face and,
before she could blink,
he started to run back
up the hill where she
had fallen.

When they reached the top, Hannah climbed off her new friend's shoulders and together they looked out into the distance. Suddenly Hannah pointed, excitedly. "There he is. There's my brother, Billy!" she said.

Hannah grew quiet and thought a long time before speaking. "Sometimes he drives me crazy, Abe, and sometimes I think that he doesn't love me," she said at last. "But you know what? He's my brother and I'm his sister, and we will love each other no matter what. I think it's time for me to go home, Abe."

Abe would be sad to see his new friend go, but he knew that she needed to be with her family and he wanted to help her. He smiled at her and sat in the snow, very close to the edge of the hill. Hannah jumped onto his huge, furry shoulders and held on tightly.

Before she knew it, Abe pushed off and they went racing down the snow-covered hill in the direction of her frantic brother. It was so much fun that she laughed and screamed with joy!

At the bottom of the hill Billy heard the noise and quickly turned see what was happening. He saw an avalanche of snow barreling toward him... an avalanche with big blue eyes! He covered his face and braced himself for the impact, but, to his surprise, there wasn't one.

When the snow finally settled, he saw his sister standing in front of him, as happy as she could be. He was so relieved to see her that he tackled her with a very big hug. "Hannah, I was so worried about you!" he cried. "Where have you been? I've been searching..."

Just then, he saw something emerging out of the
pile of snow. It was Abe. Billy froze in his place.
"H-H-Hannah...l-l-look! It's an A-A-Abominable
Snowman," he stuttered, his voice squeaking from
fear.

"Oh, him?" said Hannah, calmly looking up. "Billy, I would like you to meet my new friend, Abe. Abe helped me get home. I got lost in the woods and he found me. Abe, this is my brother, Billy."

Abe leaned forward and extended his long furry arm. He opened his hand and held out a giant finger. Trembling, Billy took hold of Abe's finger and the two shook hands. "H-hello, Abe," Billy said, using his bravest voice.

Billy suddenly felt a lot safer. He looked at his sister and managed to put a little smile on his face. "I'm so sorry I threw that snowball at you, Hannah," he said. "I just wanted to keep playing and I did the wrong thing. When I thought you were lost, I got so scared."

"It's okay, Billy. I know you didn't want to hurt my feelings. Sometimes we just make the wrong decisions. I didn't mean to scare you, either." Billy and Hannah gave each other a big hug and told each other that this would never happen again.

"Let's go home," Billy said, pulling Hannah's hand. "You go ahead," she said. "I'll be right behind you."

As Billy started to walk back toward the town, he turned and waved to Abe. "Thank you, Abe!" he shouted. "You're a good friend!" Abe waved back to him with his large hand.

"It's time for me to go, too, Abe," said Hannah. "Thank you so much for getting me home. I'll never forget you and I hope you will always be my friend." Then she removed the scarf from her neck and, reaching up, she wrapped it around his. "Merry Christmas, Abe."

Abe stood and watched as Hannah and Billy ran off into the distance. When they were out of sight, he started his journey home.

On the way back to his hill, Abe thought about his time with Hannah. It made him feel warm all over. He would never forget Hannah, either. It wasn't just her gift of the scarf. No, it was something much more special. She had given him the one thing that he truly wanted for Christmas, the gift of friendship.

Abe was thinking about these things when he walked through a line of trees into an opening in the forest where the animals were finishing up their Christmas decorating. He could tell they were having a wonderful time and he didn't want to ruin it. So, as quietly as he could, he turned to leave.

But something stopped him.

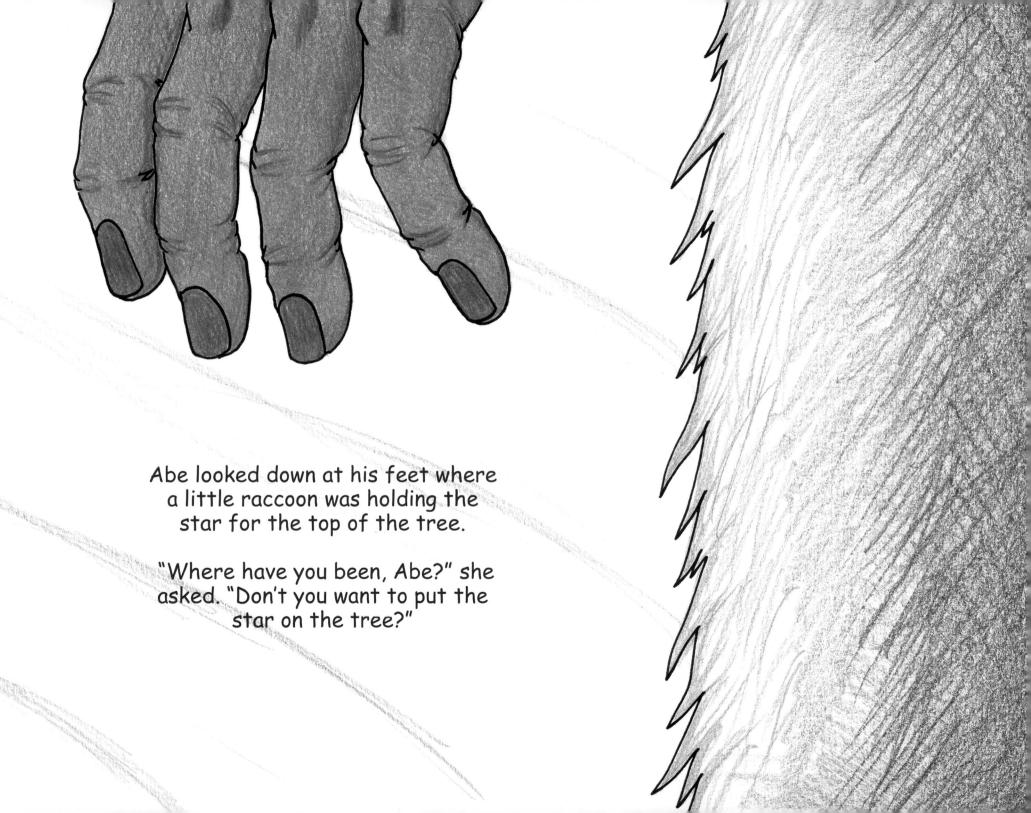

Abe looked down at his feet where
a little raccoon was holding the
star for the top of the tree.

"Where have you been, Abe?" she
asked. "Don't you want to put the
star on the tree?"

All at once, the other animals crowded around Abe and moved him toward the giant tree. A little bird flew down to take the star from the raccoon and carry it over to Abe. "Christmas Eve wouldn't be the same without you, Abe," the little bird said.

Abe could not believe his ears. He thought his friends would be glad if he were not around for Christmas Eve, but he was wrong. His friends had missed him.

So on this fine night, Abe was the happiest Abominable Snowman in the world.

THE END

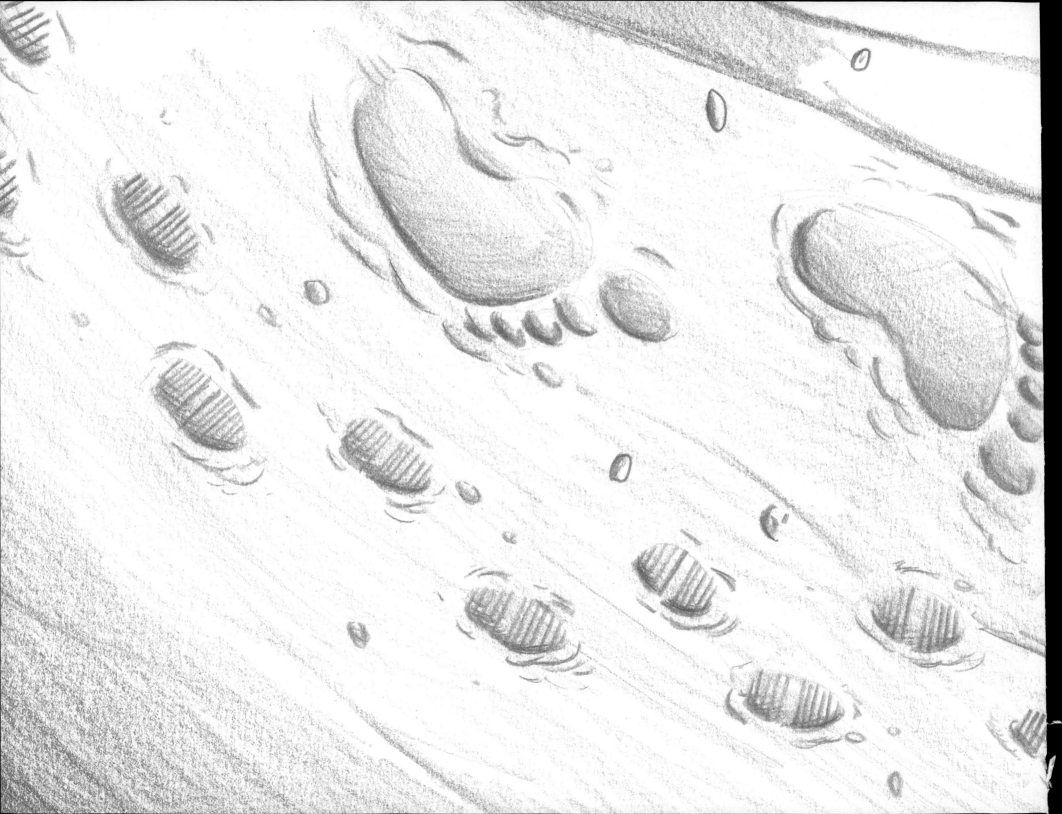